A RAKHI FOR RAKESH

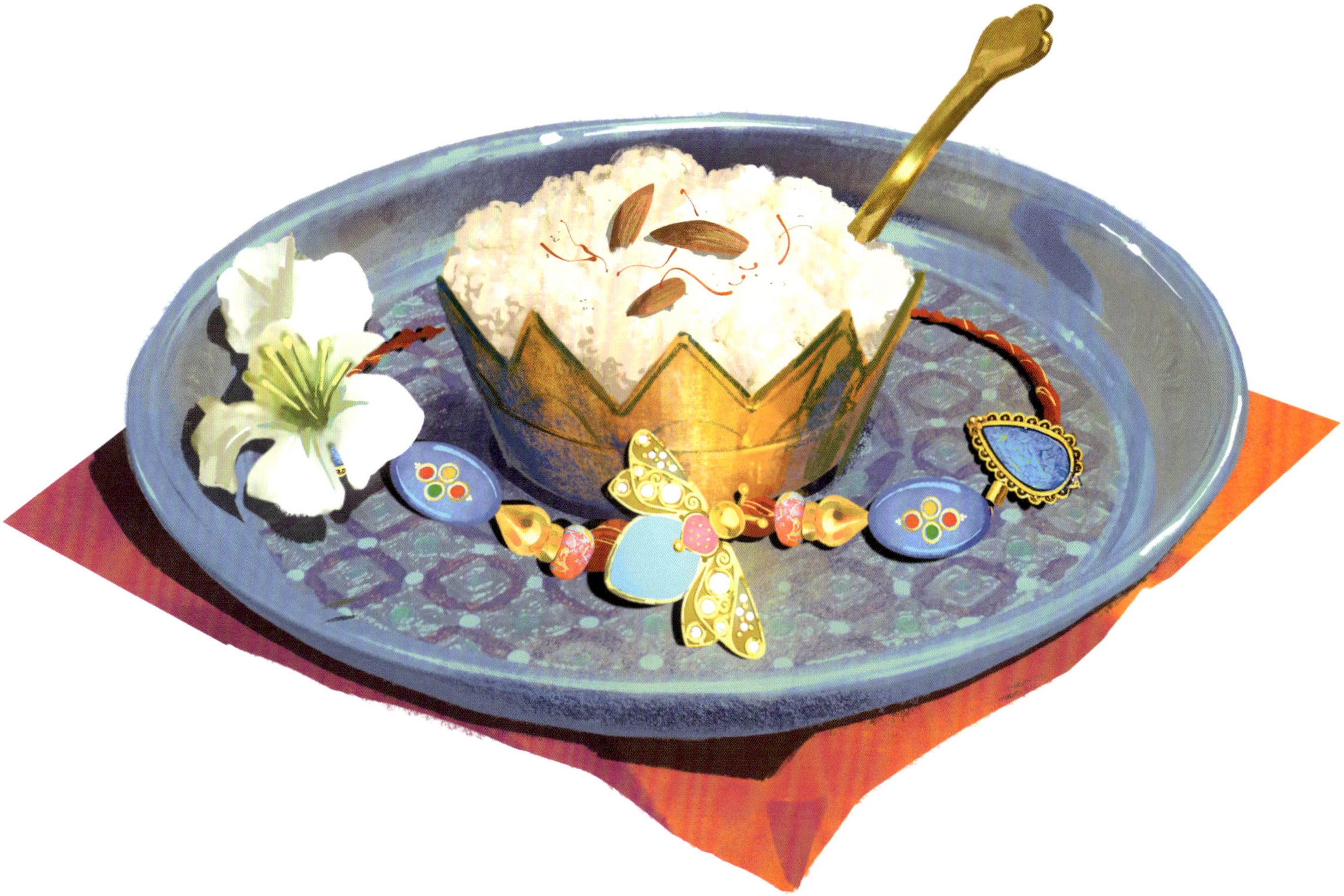

Written by Nadia Salomon • Illustrated by Nabi H. Ali

VERSIFY
An Imprint of HarperCollinsPublishers

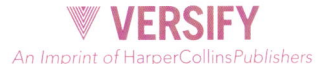

Versify is an imprint of HarperCollins Publishers.

A Rakhi for Rakesh
Text copyright © 2025 by Nadia Salomon
Illustrations copyright © 2025 by Nabi H. Ali
All rights reserved. Manufactured in Capriate San Gervasio, Italy. No part of this book may be used or reproduced in any manner whatsoever without written permission except in the case of brief quotations embodied in critical articles and reviews. For information address HarperCollins Children's Books, a division of HarperCollins Publishers, 195 Broadway, New York, NY 10007.
www.harpercollinschildrens.com

Library of Congress Control Number: 2022044838
ISBN 978-0-06-324904-2

The artist used Procreate on the iPad to create the digital illustrations for this book.
25 26 27 28 29 RTLO 10 9 8 7 6 5 4 3 2 1

First Edition

A rakhi for Superman . . .
I promise not to make you cry.
Always and forever,
N.S.A.

To Sakina Apa—for all the adventure, and for being
the best big sister anyone could ever ask for
—N.H.A.

On a good day, Aashi and her big brother, Rakesh, got along.

When they played carrom, Rakesh let Aashi go first.

When they played pirates, Aashi shared in Rakesh's treasure.

But on one *not*-so-good day . . .

Rakesh ripped Aashi's favorite drawing.
"*Sorry,* that was an *accident!*"

And when Rakesh wouldn't let Aashi play with his toy submarine . . .

"OOPS!

That was an accident, too."

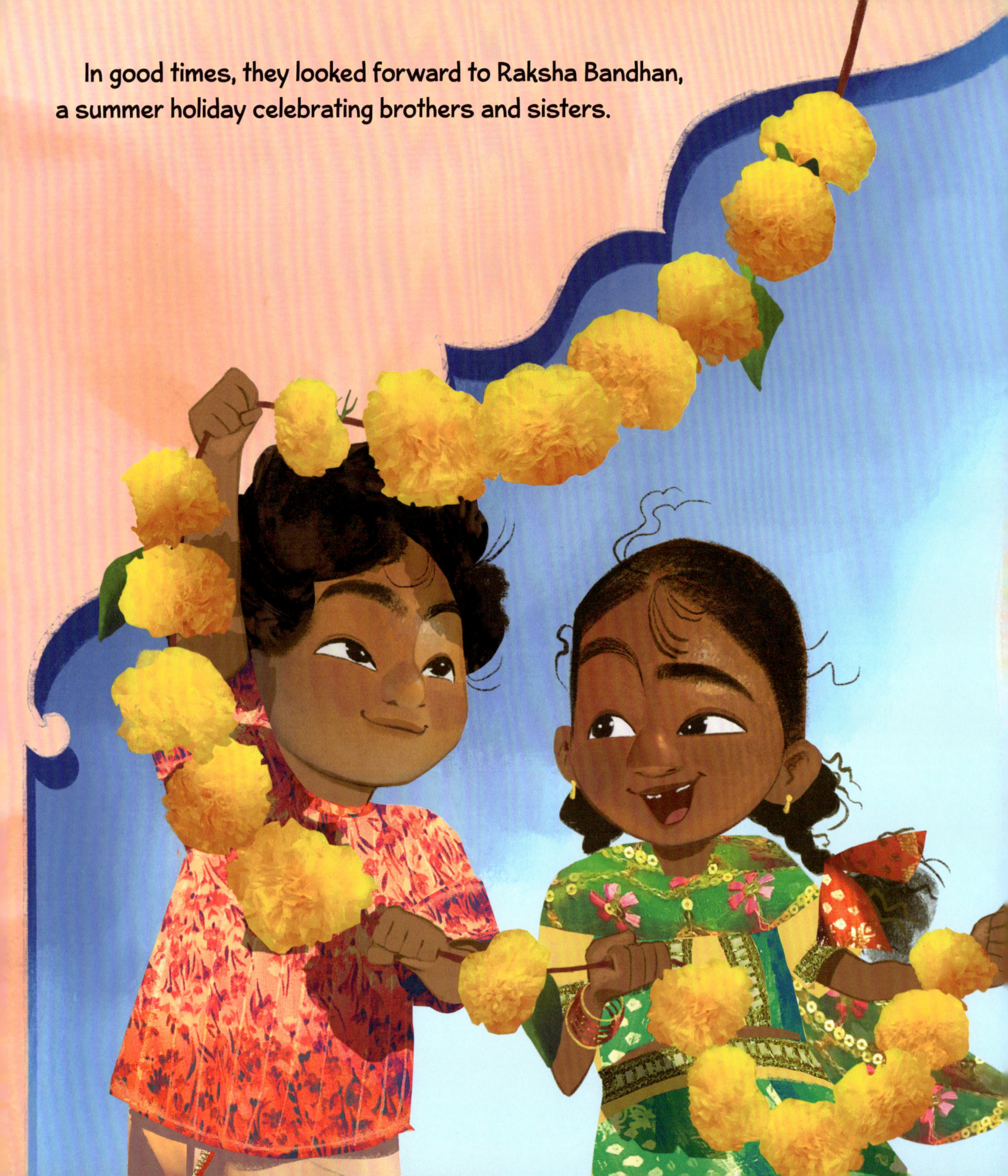

In good times, they looked forward to Raksha Bandhan, a summer holiday celebrating brothers and sisters.

Aashi and Rakesh loved making garlands, taking trips to Mr. Rao's shop, and sampling sweets before their special day. But . . .

In this *not*-so-good time, Aashi was still angry about her torn drawing. She didn't want to think about tying a rakhi on her brother's wrist.

"I wish you would go away!"

And Rakesh still raged over his broken submarine.
He didn't want to give his sister a gift in return.
"I wish I had a different sister!"

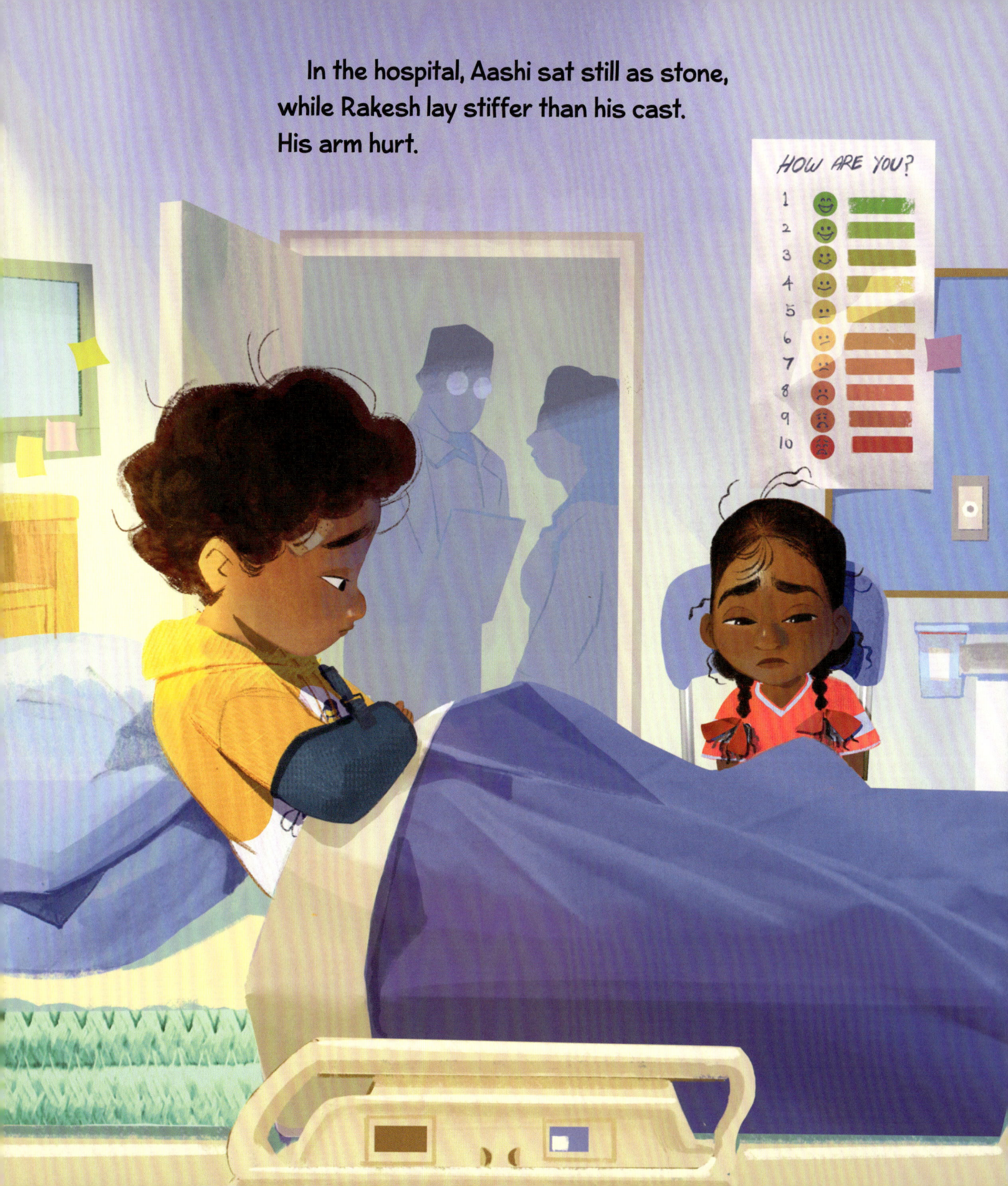

In the hospital, Aashi sat still as stone, while Rakesh lay stiffer than his cast. His arm hurt.

Only silence spoke on their way home.

The next day, Rakesh watched helplessly as Aashi strung garlands of mango leaves and marigolds.

Aashi forced a smile.

She. Missed. Rakesh.

The house was ready.
Aashi was almost ready.
Rakesh was not.

That night, Rakesh stood in the heat with a jar to collect fireflies.
Chirping crickets replaced Aashi's laughter.
He. Missed. Aashi.

Inside, Aashi scribbled here, swirled there. And after a while, she folded her drawing, then slipped it under Rakesh's door.

It made Rakesh beam.

The day before Raksha Bandhan, Aashi gathered beads, charms, and shimmery threads to make a rakhi for Rakesh.

Meanwhile, Rakesh snuck out with Nanna to buy a gift for Aashi from Mr. Rao's shop.

Aashi cut the colored silk threads in red and gold. She wove her heart into the threads she braided into a bracelet.

She tied a knot in the center—
and one on each end.

Rakesh did his best wrapping,
folding his love into each layer of tissue.

Aashi *fanned* and *fluffed* the red and gold threads,
then glued on shiny beads and charms.

Raksha Bandhan finally arrived!
A silver tray sat between the siblings.

Aashi had decorated it with fragrant flowers and Rakesh's favorite milk sweet—kova. Her rakhi crowned it.

Amma helped Aashi and Rakesh through the ceremony.

Amma lit the deepam . . .

Aashi made a wish . . .

And then Aashi slowly dabbed kumkum onto Rakesh's forehead.

Aashi's hands trembled tying the rakhi around the cast. "Does this hurt?"

Rakesh shook his head.

With eyes down, they both promised to always be there for each other.
    Then Aashi gave Rakesh the kova.

In return, Rakesh handed Aashi his gift.
Aashi tore through the tissue.

She squeezed Rakesh tight.

"I'M SORRY!"

"Jinx!" they giggled.

Then they spent the day together...
doing what they loved most.

Rakesh watched Aashi count the fireflies they had collected. Afterward, Aashi watched Rakesh twirl the rakhi around his cast.

Raksha Bandhan (Rahk·shah Bahn·dahn)

is a Hindu festival celebrated throughout India. It usually falls on a full moon day in August. During this festival, brothers and sisters celebrate their special bond. Sisters tie rakhis to their brothers' wrists and give them sweets. And brothers give gifts to their sisters in return.

A **rakhi** (rah·kee) is a colorful bracelet, usually made of red and gold silk threads. It can be decorated with beads, jewels, religious symbols, or sequins. It is also referred to as a *thread of love*.

When a sister ties the rakhi, it shows her love and heartfelt good wishes for her brother. It also signifies a brother's lifelong promise to protect his sister. And for kids with no brother, or an only female child, the tradition can be carried out with a male cousin or a close male friend—anyone considered to be like a brother. The same would be true for an only male child; the tradition can be carried out with a female cousin or close female friend considered to be like a sister.

GLOSSARY

Telugu is the language spoken in the southern Indian states of Andhra Pradesh and Telangana. It can also refer to a person from that region.

AMMA (Uhm·Mah): Mother, Mom

ANNA (Uhn·Nah): Older brother

CARROM (kar·rum): A popular board game in India played like tabletop shuffleboard

DEEPAM (dhee·puhm): A small metal or clay lamp with a cotton wick dipped in oil

KOVA (ko·vah): A grainy sweet made of condensed milk and sugar

KUMKUM (koom·koom): A red powder made of ground turmeric used for special occasions

NANNA (Nah·Nah): Father, Dad

Online resources* to learn more about Raksha Bandhan and how to make rakhis:

    www.rakhiindia.com

    www.raksha-bandhan.com

*These URLs were accurate as of the date of publishing.

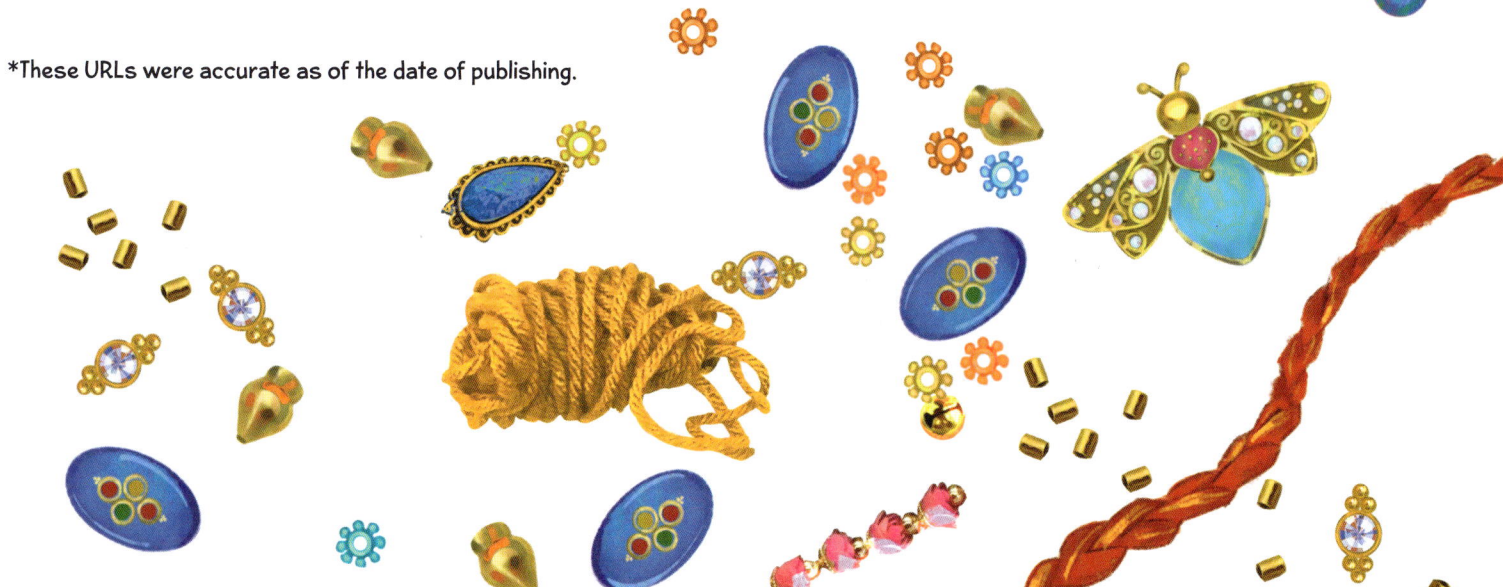